6 7 8 9 10

16 17 18 19 20

24 25 26 27

0 31 32

FiRST PUBLiSHED iN ENGLiSH 2012 BY ORDER OF THE TATE TRUSTEES
BY TATE PUBLiSHiNG, A DiViSiON OF TATE ENTERPRiSES LTD,
MiLLBANK, LONDON SW1P 4RG
WWW.TATE.ORG.UK/PUBLiSHiNG

FiRST PUBLiSHED iN PORTUGUESE AS 'CÁ EM CASA SOMOS...'
© PLANETA TANGERiNA, iSABEL MiNHÓS MARTiNS AND MADALENA MATOSO 2009
ENGLiSH LANGUAGE EDiTiON © TATE 2012

A CATALOGUE RECORD FOR THiS BOOK iS AVAiLABLE FROM THE BRiTiSH LiBRARY
iSBN 978 1 84976 049 2

DiSTRiBUTED iN THE UNiTED STATES AND CANADA BY ABRAMS, NEW YORK
LiBRARY OF CONGRESS CONTROL NUMBER: 2012936005

PRiNTED iN PORTUGAL BY PRiNTER PORTUGUESA

ISABEL MINHÓS MARTINS
MADALENA MATOSO

AT
OUR
HOUSE

TATE PUBLISHING

AT OUR HOUSE
WE HAVE 6 HEADS,
EACH ONE THINKING
ITS OWN UNIQUE
THOUGHTS...

FROM TIME TO TIME, THOUGH,
THEY ALL THINK THE SAME!

AT OUR HOUSE
WE HAVE 40 FINGERS,
10 THUMBS, 50 TOES
AND 20 CLAWS...

THAT MAKES 120 NAILS TO CLIP EVERY SUNDAY.

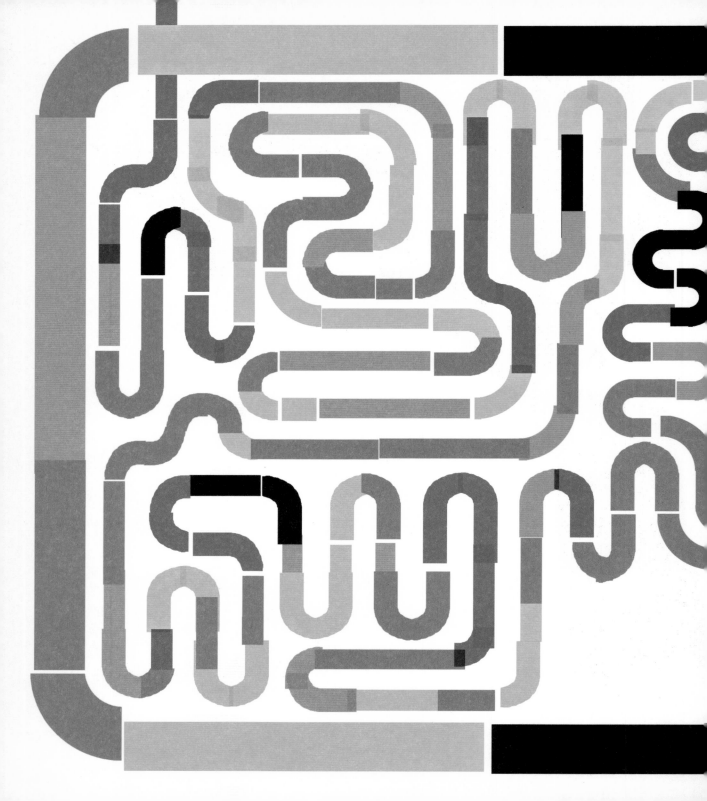

AT OUR HOUSE
WE HAVE 6 BLADDERS.
OUR INTESTINES
ARE ABOUT 60 TIMES
THE LENGTH OF AN
AVERAGE BODY...

EVERY MORNING
WE LINE UP FOR
THE SAME BATHROOM.

AT OUR HOUSE
WE HAVE 6 TUMMIES,
ALL DIFFERENT SIZES.

WHEN SUMMER COMES
WE LIKE TO SUNBATHE
ON THE BALCONY.

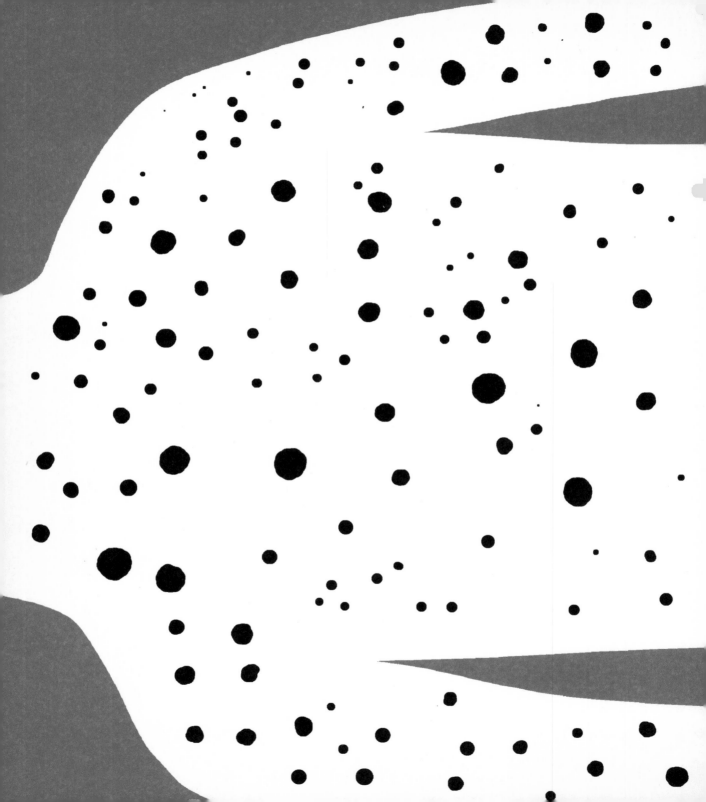

AT OUR HOUSE
WE HAVE 3,560
FRECKLES.

THERE WOULD BE
FAR FEWER
IF IT WASN'T FOR
MY FATHER'S BACK...

AT OUR HOUSE
WE HAVE 6 NOSES
AND 12 NOSTRILS.

WHEN THE FLOWERS
BLOOM, THEY ALL
ITCH AND SNEEZE.

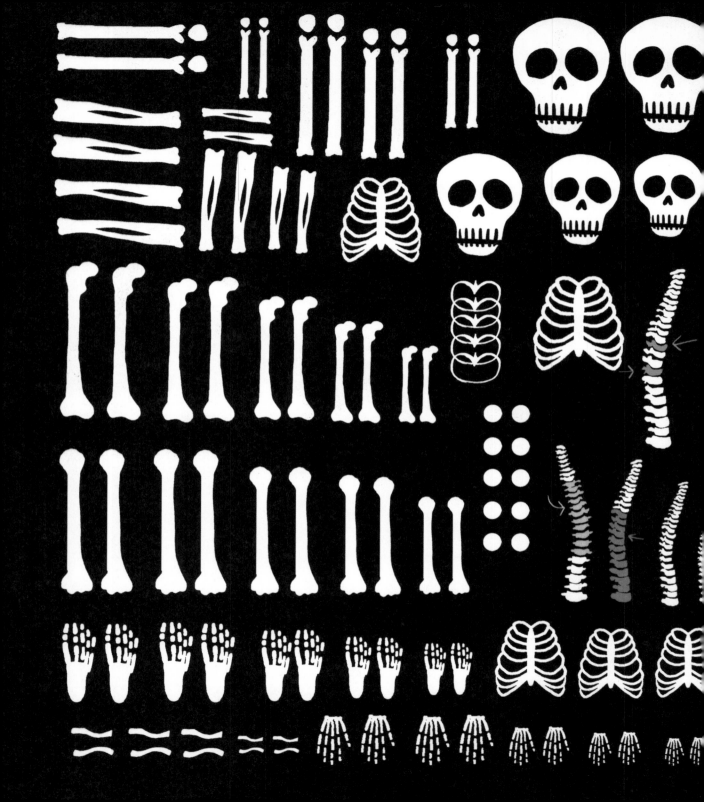

AT OUR HOUSE
WE HAVE 1,351 BONES.

DOCTOR WILLIAM HAS
TOLD US THAT WE HAVE...
191 VERTEBRAE,
146 RIBS,
12 HIP JOINTS.

...ALL IN GOOD WORKING ORDER,
THANK YOU VERY MUCH.

AT OUR HOUSE
WE HAVE
800,000 HAIRS
THAT NEED
WASHING, DRYING
AND UNTANGLING.

WHEN SPRING ARRIVES,
WE LIKE TO CUT OUR
HAIR SHORTER.

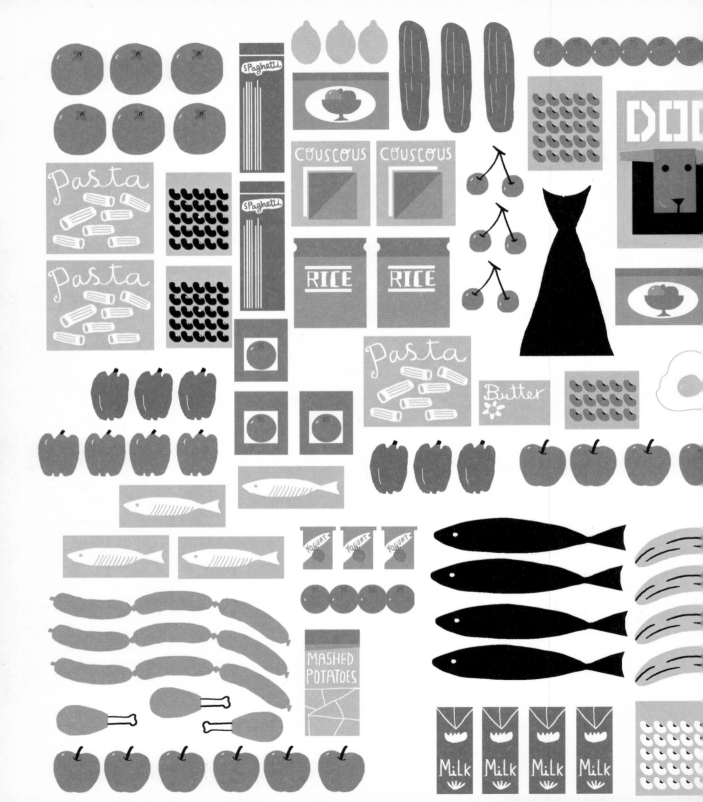

AT OUR HOUSE
WE HAVE
6 MOUTHS,
6 TONGUES
AND 168 TEETH.

MY GRANDFATHER
SAYS THAT
WE TALK LIKE
CROWS AND EAT
LIKE LIONS.

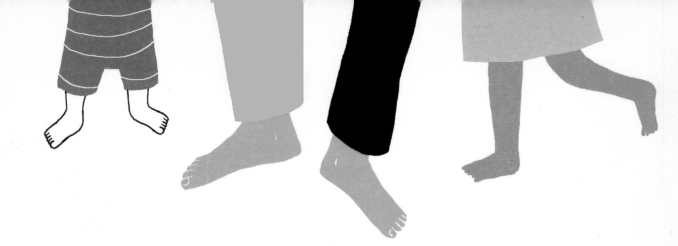

AT OUR HOUSE
WE HAVE 5 PAIRS
OF LEGS, 4 PAWS
AND 10 FEET.

THAT MEANS...
10 SHOES TO TAKE OFF AT THE END
OF THE DAY... 10 SOCKS TO THROW
INTO A CORNER...

AND, SOMETIMES, ONLY 2 HANDS TO PICK
UP ALL THE MESS.

AT OUR HOUSE WE ARE 6.

BUT ON HOLIDAYS
WE QUICKLY BECOME 16.
THE DOORBELL RINGS
AND SOON WE ARE 27.
COUSINS ARRIVE AND
SUDDENLY WE ARE 32...

WE BEGiN
COUNTiNG...
AT OUR HOUSE WE NOW HAVE
32 HEADS
240 FiNGERS
60 THUMBS
ALMOST A QUARTER OF
A MiLE OF INTESTINES

32 TUMMIES
(BIG AND SMALL)
32 NOSES
68 LEGS
8 PAWS
6,822 BONES
MORE THAN
FOUR MILLION HAIRS
924 TEETH AND 32 TONGUES...
... CHEWING AND TALKING NONSTOP.

2 EYES

1 MOUTH

ADULTS: 32 TEETH

CHILDREN: +- 20 TEETH

A SWALLOWED PIECE OF FOOD TAKES ABOUT 5 SECONDS TO REACH THE STOMACH

1 NOSE
2 NOSTRILS

ON AVERAGE WE BREATHE BETWEEN 720 AND 1,200 TIMES EVERY HOUR

150,000

2 EARS

THAN 0.3 % OF THE TOTAL BODY WEIGHT